HENRY

Based on *The Railway Series* by the Rev. W. Awdry

Illustrations by

Robin Davies and Jerry Smith

EGMONT

3
5
Annie

EGMONT

We bring stories to life

First published in Great Britain in 2005
by Egmont UK Limited
239 Kensington High Street, London W8 6SA

HiT entertainment

ISBN 978 1 4052 1712 5
5 7 9 10 8 6 4
Printed in Great Britain

The Forest Stewardship Council (FSC) is an international, non-governmental organisation dedicated to promoting responsible management of the world's forests. FSC operates a system of forest certification and product labelling that allows consumers to identify wood and wood-based products from well managed forests.

For more information about Egmont's paper buying policy please visit www.egmont.co.uk/ethicalpublishing

For more information about the FSC please visit their website at www.fsc.uk.org

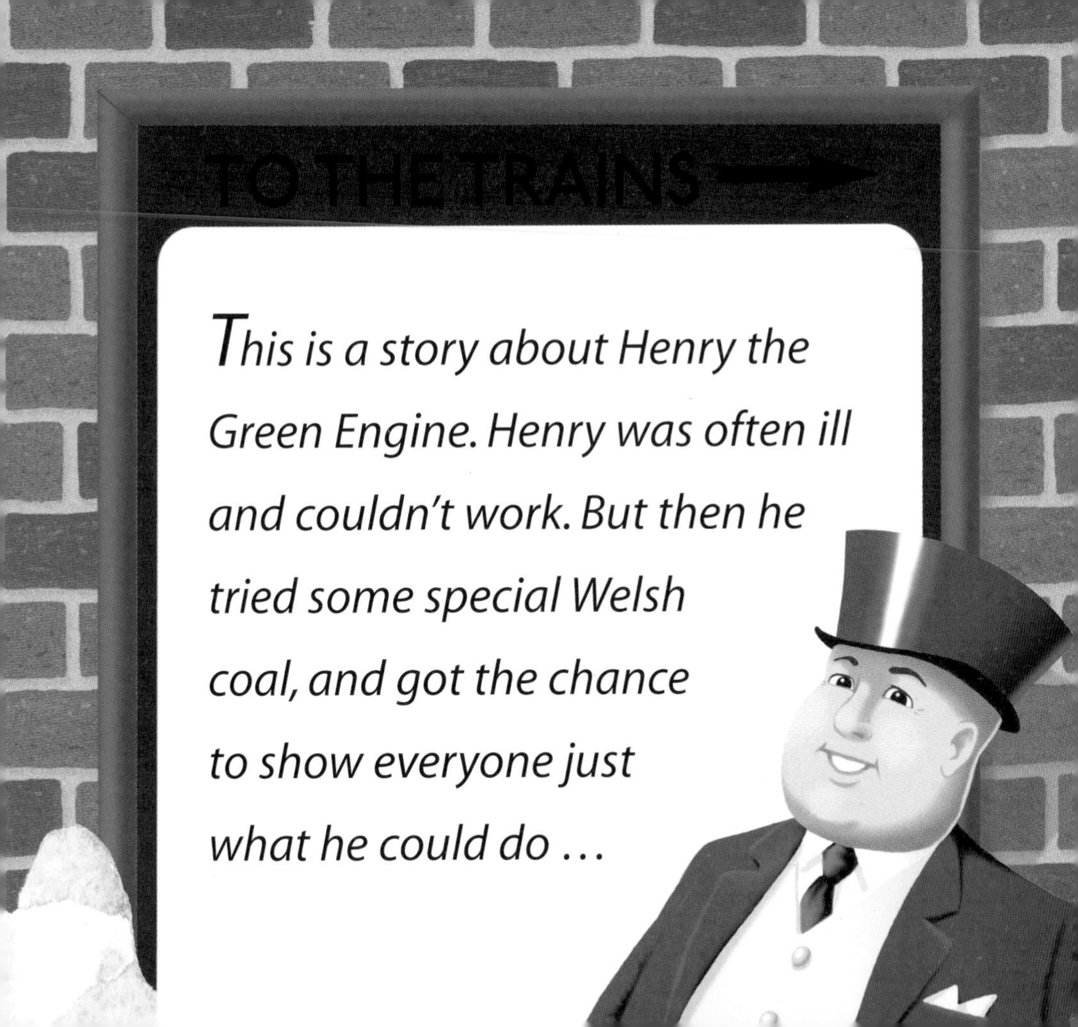

This is a story about Henry the Green Engine. Henry was often ill and couldn't work. But then he tried some special Welsh coal, and got the chance to show everyone just what he could do . . .

Henry was a big engine. Sometimes he could pull trains, but sometimes he felt too weak, and had to stay in the yard.

One morning, Henry was feeling very sorry for himself.

"I suffer dreadfully, and no one cares," he said.

"Rubbish, Henry," snorted James. "You don't work hard enough!"

The Fat Controller spoke to Henry.

"You're too expensive, Henry," he said. "You have had lots of new parts and a new coat of paint, but they have done you no good. If we can't make you better, we will have to get another engine instead of you."

This made Henry, his Driver and his Fireman very sad.

The Fat Controller was waiting when Henry came to the platform. He had taken off his hat and coat and put on overalls. He climbed on to Henry's footplate.

Henry managed to start, but his Fireman was not happy.

"Henry is a bad steamer," he told The Fat Controller. "I build up his fire, but it doesn't give enough heat."

Henry tried very hard to pull the train, but it was no good. He didn't have enough steam. He gradually came to a stop outside Edward's station.

"Oh dear," thought Henry. "Now I shall be sent away. Oh dear. Oh dear."

Henry went slowly into a siding, and Edward took charge of the train.

"What do you think is wrong, Fireman?" asked The Fat Controller.

"It's the coal, Sir," he answered. "It hasn't been very good lately. The other engines can manage because they have big fireboxes, but Henry's is small and can't make enough heat. With Welsh coal he'd be a different engine."

"It's expensive," said The Fat Controller, "but Henry must have a fair chance. I'll send James to fetch some."

Henry's Driver and Fireman were very excited when the coal came.

"Now we'll show them, Henry, old fellow," they said.

They carefully oiled Henry's joints, and polished his brass until it shone like gold.

Henry felt very proud.

3

Then Henry's Fireman carefully made his fire. He put large lumps of coal like a wall around the outside of the fire. Then he covered the glowing middle part with smaller lumps.

"You're spoiling my fire," complained Henry.

"Wait and see," said the Fireman. "We'll have a roaring fire just when we need it."

The Fireman was right. When Henry reached the platform, the water was boiling nicely, and he had to let off steam. "Wheeeesh!"

"How are you, Henry?" asked The Fat Controller.

"Peep! Peep! Peep!" whistled Henry. "I feel fine!"

"Do you have a good fire, Driver?" The Fat Controller asked.

"Never better, Sir, and plenty of steam," he replied.

3

Henry was impatient. He wanted to set off.

"No record breaking," warned The Fat Controller. "Don't push him too hard, Driver."

"Henry won't need pushing, Sir," the Driver replied. "I'll have to hold him back!"

Henry had a lovely day. He had never felt so well in his life. He wanted to go fast, but his Driver wouldn't let him.

"Steady, old fellow," he said. "There's plenty of time."

3

But still, Henry went quite fast, and they arrived at the station early.

Thomas puffed in.

"Where have you been, lazy bones?" asked Henry.

But before Thomas could answer, Henry was off again. "I can't wait for slow tank engines like you," he said. "Goodbye!" And off he sped.

"Gosh!" said Thomas to Annie and Clarabel. "Have you ever seen anything like it?"

Annie and Clarabel agreed that they never had.

Henry was very happy. With his new Welsh coal, he could work as hard as the other engines.

Then one day, Henry had a crash and The Fat Controller sent him to be mended. Workmen gave Henry a brand new shape, and a bigger firebox, so he wouldn't need special coal any more.

Now Henry is so splendid and strong, he sometimes pulls the Express.

"Peep! Peep! Pippippeep!" whistles Henry happily.

3
5
Annie

The Thomas Story Library is THE definitive collection of stories about Thomas and ALL his friends.

There are now 50 stories from the Island of Sodor to collect!

So go on, start your Thomas Story Library NOW!

Cut along the dotted line

A Fantastic Offer for Thomas the Tank Engine Fans!

In every Thomas Story Library book like this one, you will find a special token. Collect 6 Thomas tokens and we will send you a brilliant Thomas poster, and a double-sided bedroom door hanger! Simply tape a £1 coin in the space above, and fill out the form overleaf.

TO BE COMPLETED BY AN ADULT

To apply for this great offer, ask an adult to complete the coupon below and send it with a pound coin and 6 tokens, to:
THOMAS OFFERS, PO BOX 715, HORSHAM RH12 5WG

☐ Please send a Thomas poster and door hanger. I enclose 6 tokens plus a £1 coin. (Price includes P&P)

Fan's name...

Address...

....Postcode..............................

Date of birth...

Name of parent/guardian...

Signature of parent/guardian...

Please allow 28 days for delivery. Offer is only available while stocks last. We reserve the right to change the terms of this offer at any time and we offer a 14 day money back guarantee. This does not affect your statutory rights.

☐ Data Protection Act: If you do not wish to receive other similar offers from us or companies we recommend, please tick this box. Offers apply to UK only.

Cut along the dotted line